ASTERIX AND THE LAUREL WREATH

TEXT BY GOSCINNY

DRAWINGS BY UDERZO

TRANSLATED BY ANTHEA BELL AND DEREK HOCKRIDGE

HODDER DARGAUD
LONDON SYDNEY AUCKLAND

ASTERIX IN OTHER COUNTRIES

Australia Hodder Dargaud, 2 Apollo Place, Lane Cove, New South Wales 2066
Austria Delta Verlag, Postfach 1215, 7 Stuttgart 1, G.F.R.
Belgium Dargaud Bénélux, 3 rue Kindermans, 1050 Brussels
Brazil Cedibra, rua Filomena Nunes 162, Rio de Janeiro
Canada Dargaud Canada, 307 Benjamin-Hudon, St. Laurent, Montreal P.Q. H4N1J1
Denmark Gutenberghus Bladene, Vognmagergade 11, 1148 Copenhagen K
Finland Sanoma Osakeyhtio, Ludviginkatu 2–10, 00130 Helsinki 13
France Regional Editions
(Langue d'Oc) Société Toulousaine du Livre, Avenue de Larrieu, 31094 Toulouse
German Federal Republic Delta Verlag, Postfach 1215, 7 Stuttgart 1, G.F.R.
Greece Anglo-Hellenic Agency, Kriezotou 3, Syntagma, Athens 134, Greece
Holland Dargaud Bénélux, 3 rue Kindermans, 1050 Brussels, Belgium
(Distribution) Oberon, Ceylonpoort 5–25, Haarlem, Holland
Hong Kong Hodder Dargaud, c/o United Publishers Service Private Ltd, Stanhope House, 734 King's Road
Iceland Fjolvi HF, Njorvasund 15a, Reykjavik
Indonesia Pt Sinar Kasih, Tromolpos 260, Jakarta
Israel Dahlia Pelled Publishers, P.O. Box 33325, Tel Aviv
Italy Arnoldo Mondadori Editore, 1 Via Belvedere, 37131 Verona
Latin America Grijalbo-Dargaud S.A., Deu y Mata 98–102, Barcelona 29
New Zealand Hodder Dargaud, P.O. Box 3858, Auckland 1
Norway A/S Hjemmet (Gutenburghus Group), Kristian den 4des Gate 13, Oslo 1
Portugal Meriberica, rua D. Filipa de Vilherna 4–5°, Lisbon 1
Roman Empire *(Latin)* Delta Verlag, Postfach 1215, 7 Stuttgart 1, G.F.R.
South Africa *(English)* Hodder Dargaud, P.O. Box 32213, Braamfontein Centre, Braamfontein 2017 Johannesburg
Spain Grijalbo-Dargaud S.A., Deu y Mata 98–102, Barcelona 29
Sweden Hemmets Journal Forlag (Gutenburghes Group), Fack, 200 22 Malmo
Switzerland Interpress Dargaud, En Budron B, 1052 Le Mont/Lausanne
Turkey Kervan Kitabcilik, Serefendi Sokagi 31, Cagaloglu-Istanbul
Wales *(Welsh)* Gwasg Y Dref Wen, 28 Church Road, Yr Eglwys Newydd, Cardiff CF4 2EA
Yugoslavia Nip Forum, Vojvode Misica 1–3, 2100 Novi Sad

— Asterix and the Laurel Wreath —

ISBN 0 340 19107 4 (cased edition)
ISBN 0 340 20699 3 (paperbound edition)

First published in Great Britain 1974 (cased)
Sixth impression 1979

First published in Great Britain 1976 (paperbound)
Seventh impression 1981

Printed in Italy for Hodder Dargaud
Mill Road, Dunton Green, Sevenoaks, Kent
by F. lli Pagano S.p.A. – Genoa, Campomorone

The year is 50 BC. Gaul is entirely occupied by the Romans. Well, not entirely... One small village of indomitable Gauls still holds out against the invaders. And life is not easy for the Roman legionaries who garrison the fortified camps of Totorum, Aquarium, Laudanum and Compendium...

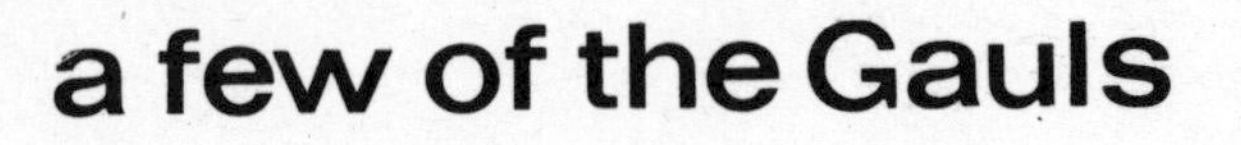

a few of the Gauls

Asterix, the hero of these adventures. A shrewd, cunning little warrior; all perilous missions are immediately entrusted to him. Asterix gets his superhuman strength from the magic potion brewed by the druid Getafix...

Obelix, Asterix's inseparable friend. A menhir delivery-man by trade; addicted to wild boar. Obelix is always ready to drop everything and go off on a new adventure with Asterix – so long as there's wild boar to eat, and plenty of fighting.

Getafix, the venerable village druid. Gathers mistletoe and brews magic potions. His speciality is the potion which gives the drinker superhuman strength. But Getafix also has other recipes up his sleeve...

Cacofonix, the bard. Opinion is divided as to his musical gifts. Cacofonix thinks he's a genius. Everyone else thinks he's unspeakable. But so long as he doesn't speak, let alone sing, everybody likes him...

Finally, Vitalstatistix, the chief of the tribe. Majestic, brave and hot-tempered, the old warrior is respected by his men and feared by his enemies. Vitalstatistix himself has only one fear; he is afraid the sky may fall on his head tomorrow. But as he always says, 'Tomorrow never comes.'

ANOTHER SUNNY DAY HAS JUST DAWNED UPON THE GREATEST CITY IN THE UNIVERSE-
ROME.
ALTHOUGH, BY CAESAR'S DECREE, TRAFFIC IS NOT ALLOWED ON THE STREETS IN THE DAYTIME, THE CITY IS INCREDIBLY NOISY, CROWDED WITH SHOPKEEPERS AND STREETSELLERS CRYING THEIR WARES... FRUCTUARII, PEPONARII, OLITORES, PISCATORES, VINARII, SILIGINARII, PASTILLARII...
EAT MORE FRUIT!
RIPE JUICY MELONS!
TRY MY VEGETABLES! NICE WHOLESOME VEG!
FISH! GOOD FRESH FISH!
CAKES!
SWEETS!
THE PASSERS-BY ARE BESET BY BEGGARS AND FLAG SELLERS...
HAVE PITY ON A POOR GLADIATOR IN REDUCED CIRCUMSTANCES!
DON'T YOU WANT TO SUPPORT A GOOD CAUSE THEN?
TOURISTS FROM ALL OVER THE WORLD, THRACIANS, GOTHS, BRITONS, EGYPTIANS, SICAMBRES, ETHIOPIANS, NUMIDIANS, ALL ADD TO THE LOCAL COLOUR...
AND HERE WE HAVE THE CIRCUS MAXIMUS...
AND HERE WE HAVE THE CIRCUS MAXIMUS...
and here we have the Circus Maximus
IN FACT, EVERYTHING LEADS US TO BELIEVE THAT WE MAY SEE EVEN STRANGER SIGHTS AROUND THE NEXT CORNER...

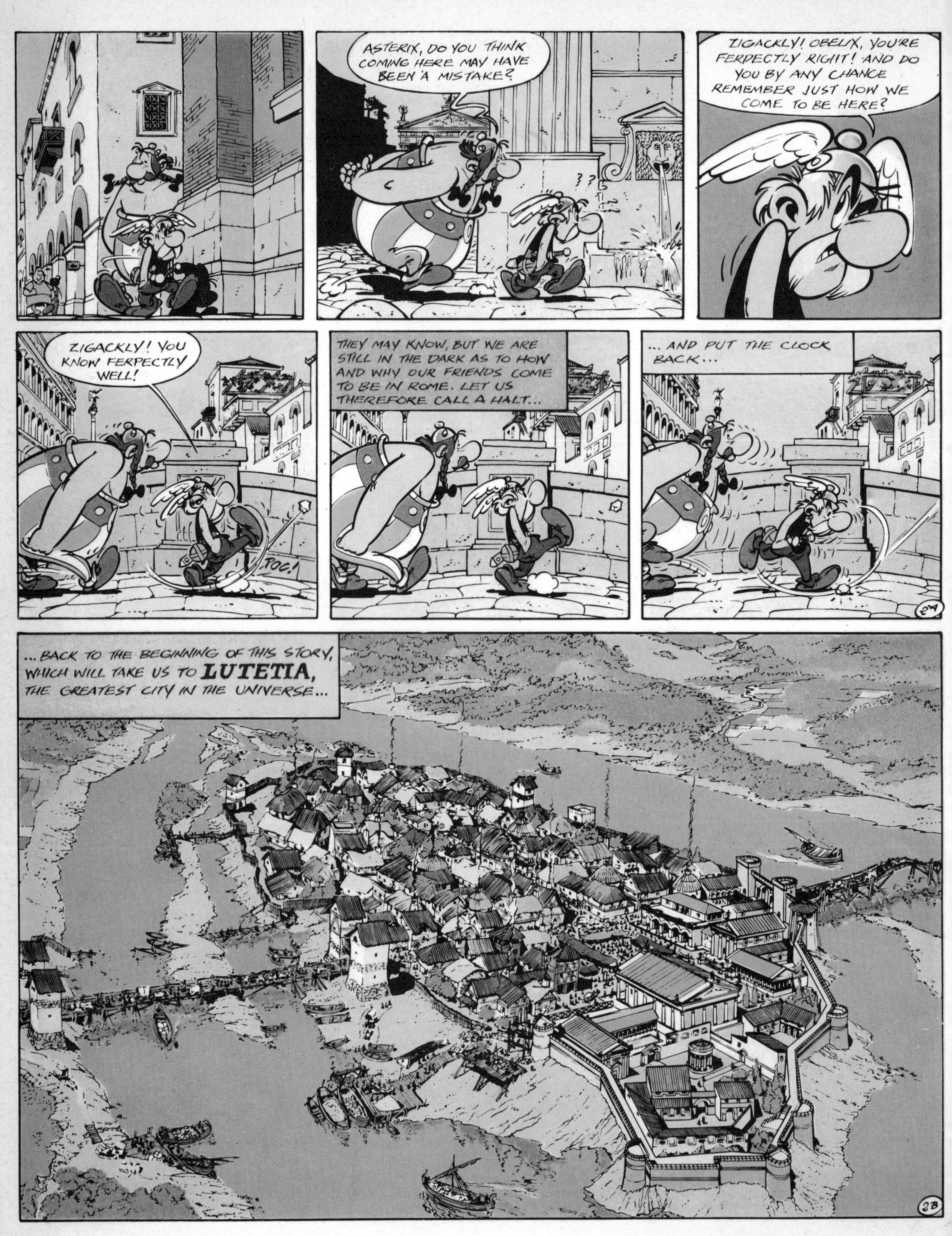
ASTERIX, DO YOU THINK COMING HERE MAY HAVE BEEN A MISTAKE?
? ?
ZIGACKLY! OBELIX, YOU'RE FERPECTLY RIGHT! AND DO YOU BY ANY CHANCE REMEMBER JUST HOW WE COME TO BE HERE?
ZIGACKLY! YOU KNOW FERPECTLY WELL!
POC!
THEY MAY KNOW, BUT WE ARE STILL IN THE DARK AS TO HOW AND WHY OUR FRIENDS COME TO BE IN ROME. LET US THEREFORE CALL A HALT...
... AND PUT THE CLOCK BACK...
... BACK TO THE BEGINNING OF THIS STORY, WHICH WILL TAKE US TO LUTETIA, THE GREATEST CITY IN THE UNIVERSE...

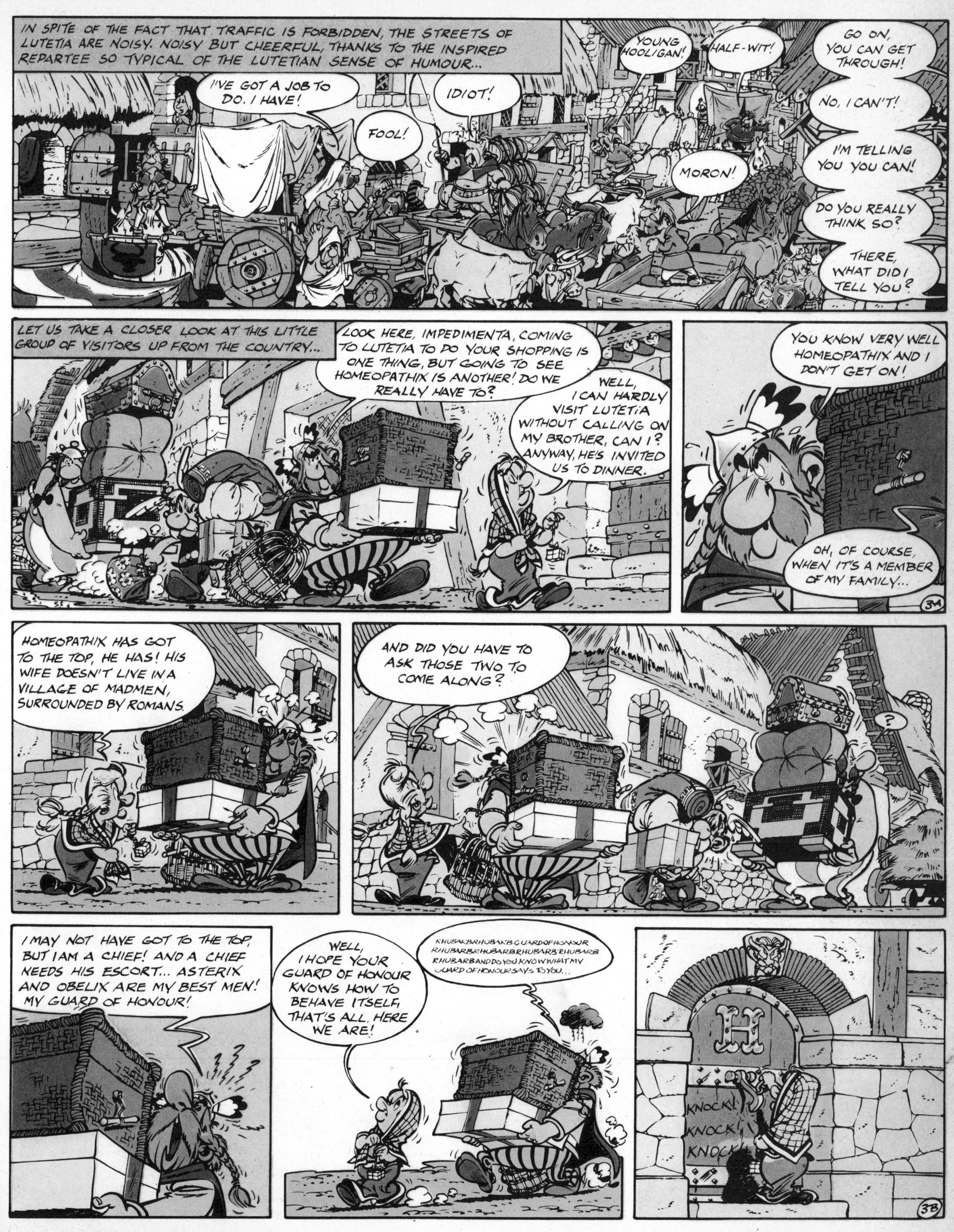
IN SPITE OF THE FACT THAT TRAFFIC IS FORBIDDEN, THE STREETS OF LUTETIA ARE NOISY. NOISY BUT CHEERFUL, THANKS TO THE INSPIRED REPARTEE SO TYPICAL OF THE LUTETIAN SENSE OF HUMOUR...
I'VE GOT A JOB TO DO. I HAVE!
FOOL!
IDIOT!
YOUNG HOOLIGAN!
HALF-WIT!
MORON!
GO ON, YOU CAN GET THROUGH!
NO, I CAN'T!
I'M TELLING YOU YOU CAN!
DO YOU REALLY THINK SO?
THERE, WHAT DID I TELL YOU?
LET US TAKE A CLOSER LOOK AT THIS LITTLE GROUP OF VISITORS UP FROM THE COUNTRY...
LOOK HERE, IMPEDIMENTA, COMING TO LUTETIA TO DO YOUR SHOPPING IS ONE THING, BUT GOING TO SEE HOMEOPATHIX IS ANOTHER! DO WE REALLY HAVE TO?
WELL, I CAN HARDLY VISIT LUTETIA WITHOUT CALLING ON MY BROTHER, CAN I? ANYWAY, HE'S INVITED US TO DINNER.
YOU KNOW VERY WELL HOMEOPATHIX AND I DON'T GET ON!
OH, OF COURSE, WHEN IT'S A MEMBER OF MY FAMILY...
HOMEOPATHIX HAS GOT TO THE TOP, HE HAS! HIS WIFE DOESN'T LIVE IN A VILLAGE OF MADMEN, SURROUNDED BY ROMANS.
AND DID YOU HAVE TO ASK THOSE TWO TO COME ALONG?
?
I MAY NOT HAVE GOT TO THE TOP, BUT I AM A CHIEF! AND A CHIEF NEEDS HIS ESCORT... ASTERIX AND OBELIX ARE MY BEST MEN! MY GUARD OF HONOUR!
WELL, I HOPE YOUR GUARD OF HONOUR KNOWS HOW TO BEHAVE ITSELF, THAT'S ALL. HERE WE ARE!
RHUBARBRHUBARB GUARDOFHONOUR RHUBARBRHUBARBRHUBARBRHUBARB RHUBARBANDDOYOUKNOWWHATMY GUARDOFHONOURSAYSTOYOU...
H
KNOCK! KNOCK! KNOCK

LITTLE F DIMENTA!
HOMEOPATHIKINS!
TAPIOCA! TAPIOCA! IMPEDIMENTA AND WHATSIS NAME HAVE ARRIVED!
WHATSISNAME? WHAT DO YOU MEAN, WHATSISNAME?
I'VE BROUGHT YOU ONE OF OUR SEASIDE SHELLS... VITALSTATISTIX WANTED TO BRING YOU A MENHIR, THE SAME AS USUAL.
BUT MY DEAR CHAP, WHERE AM I GOING TO PUT THESE MENHIRS OF YOURS?
YOU REALLY WANT ME TO TELL YOU?
VITALSTA-TISTIX!
OH, HOW LOVELY IT IS HERE!
YES, I'VE REDECORATED THE WHOLE PLACE. I WAS GETTING TIRED OF COUNTRY STUFF... TAPIOCA, LET'S HAVE A DRINK.
TRY SOME OF THE 55 B.C., FROM OUR OWN VINEYARD. IT'S A MODEST, UNPRETENTIOUS LITTLE WINE, BUT I HOPE YOU LIKE IT.
HOW'S BUSINESS, HOMEOPATHIX? STILL GOOD?
EXCELLENT! I'M ABOUT TO OPEN BRANCHES AT LUGDUNUM AND MASSILIA...
HOW FASCINATING! AND WILL YOU BE DOING MUCH TRAVELLING?
NOT IF I CAN HELP IT! WHEN A MAN IS TIRED OF LUTETIA, HE IS TIRED OF LIFE. THE REST OF GAUL IS ONLY FIT FOR BOARS
LET'S HAVE SOME MORE OF THE 55 B.C., OBELIX. AT LEAST THAT'S MODEST AND UNPRETENTIOUS.
?

CENA IS SERVED!
OH, TAPIOCA, HOW WONDERFUL!
OF COURSE, IT MUST BE A BIT OF A CHANGE FROM THE STUFF YOU GET TO EAT AT HOME!
AND WHAT'S WRONG WITH WHAT WE GET TO EAT AT HOME?
NOTHING, EXCEPT I DON'T OFTEN HAVE BEAVERS' TAILS IN STRAWBERRY SAUCE AT HOME!
HEY, OBELIX! PASS THE WINE, WILL YOU?
NOW, WHATSYOURNAME, HOW ABOUT SOME COW'S HOOF MOULD? I BET YOU'VE NEVER HAD ANYTHING LIKE THIS...
YOU DON'T IMPRESS ME WITH YOUR COW'S HOOF MOULD! YOU'RE JUST MAKING PIGS OF YOURSELVES!
VITALSTATISTIX, DON'T BE SUCH A BOOR!
WELL, AT LEAST I CAN BRING HOME THE BACON!
HOMEOPATHIX!
DID MADAM CALL?
YES. MORE WINE, PLEASE.
WELL, I MAY NOT HAVE YOUR MONEY, BUT I DO HAVE HONOUR AND GLORY INSTEAD!
AND DOES HONOUR AND GLORY PROVIDE YOU WITH COW'S HOOF MOULD, DEAR BROTHER-IN-LAW?

HONOUR AND GLORY IS WORTH A LOT MORE THAN FOW'S COOF... I MEAN HOW'S MOOF... I MEAN ALL THIS ROT!
YOU COME TO MY VILLAGE, YOU AND SEMOLINA... TAPIOCA! I'LL GIVE YOU A MEAL. AND WHAT A MEAL! ONE YOUR MONEY COULD NEVER BUY! HIC!
AND WHAT EXACTLY WILL THIS GOURMET MEAL CONSIST OF?
AHA! A STEW... OUT-OF-THIS-WORLD... SEASONED WITH...
CAESONED WITH CAESAR'S LAUREL WREATH! HIC!
PRRFFFF!
TAKE NO NOTICE. HE'S HAD A DROP TOO MUCH.
THAT'S ALL RIGHT, IMPEDIMENTA. HE'S VERY AMUSING.
AMUSING, EH? HIC! ALL RIGHT THEN, YOU WAIT AND SEE! I'M SENDING MY MEN TO ROME TO BRING ME CAESAR'S LAUREL WREATH, TO SEASON THE STEW I SHALL GIVE YOU WHEN YOU VISIT MY VILLAGE!
ZIGACKLY! WHATSISNAME ISH FERPECTLY RIGHT! HIC!
?!?
LET GO OF ME, ASTERIX! WE'RE GOING TO ROME TO BRING BACK CHAESHAR'S LAUREL WREATH! ZIGACTLY!
COME TO MY ARMS, OBELIX!
HOMEOPATHIKINS!
NO! SINCE THIS BIGHEADED WARRIOR OF YOURS IS SO CLEVER, I'LL ACCEPT HIS INVITATION!
BUT I HAVE HIS WORD OF HONOUR THAT IT REALLY WILL BE CAESAR'S LAUREL WREATH IN THE STEW, DON'T I?
THASH FERPECTLY RIGHT!
IMPEDIMENTA, DARLING... D-DID YOU SEE ANYTHING NICE IN LUTETIA?

HIC!
BOOHOOOOO! I'VE NEVER BEEN SO HUMILIATED. AND THOSE DRUNKARDS JUST SAY ANY OLD THING THAT COMES INTO THEIR MINDS...
WHAT DO YOU MEAN, ANY OLD THING? HE SHALL HAVE A STEW SEASONED WITH CAESAR'S LAUREL WR...
IMPEDIMENTA IS QUITE RIGHT. IT WAS A RIDICULOUS THING TO...
THERE! YOU SEE? EVEN YOUR BEST MEN THINK YOU'RE A GREAT FOOL OF A BOORISH OLD...
OH, I NEVER SAID I THOUGHT...
ALL RIGHT THEN, IF YOU DIDN'T, YOU CAN SET OFF FOR ROME STRAIGHT AWAY AND BRING ME BACK CAESAR'S LAUREL WREATH!
ZIGACKLY!
COME TO MY ARMS!
DO YOU KNOW WHAT TIME IT IS? TAKE YOUR GIRL FRIEND SOME-WHERE ELSE, YOU DECADENT LOT!
AND NOW THAT WE KNOW HOW AND WHY ASTERIX AND OBELIX LANDED UP IN ROME, LET US GO ON WITH OUR STORY...
IT'S ALL YOUR FAULT! AND ALL I'VE GOT IS A GOURD OF MAGIC POTION THAT GETAFIX THE DRUID GAVE ME... IT'S NOT MUCH, ON THIS KIND OF EXPEDITION!
POC!
YOU'RE RIGHT, I DID HAVE A DROP TOO MUCH TO DRINK... STILL, IT WON'T BE ALL THAT DIFFICULT. WE MARCH INTO CAESAR'S PALACE, WE PICK UP THE LAUREL WREATH, AND WE GO BACK HOME. SIMPLE, REALLY.
OH, FERDECT!

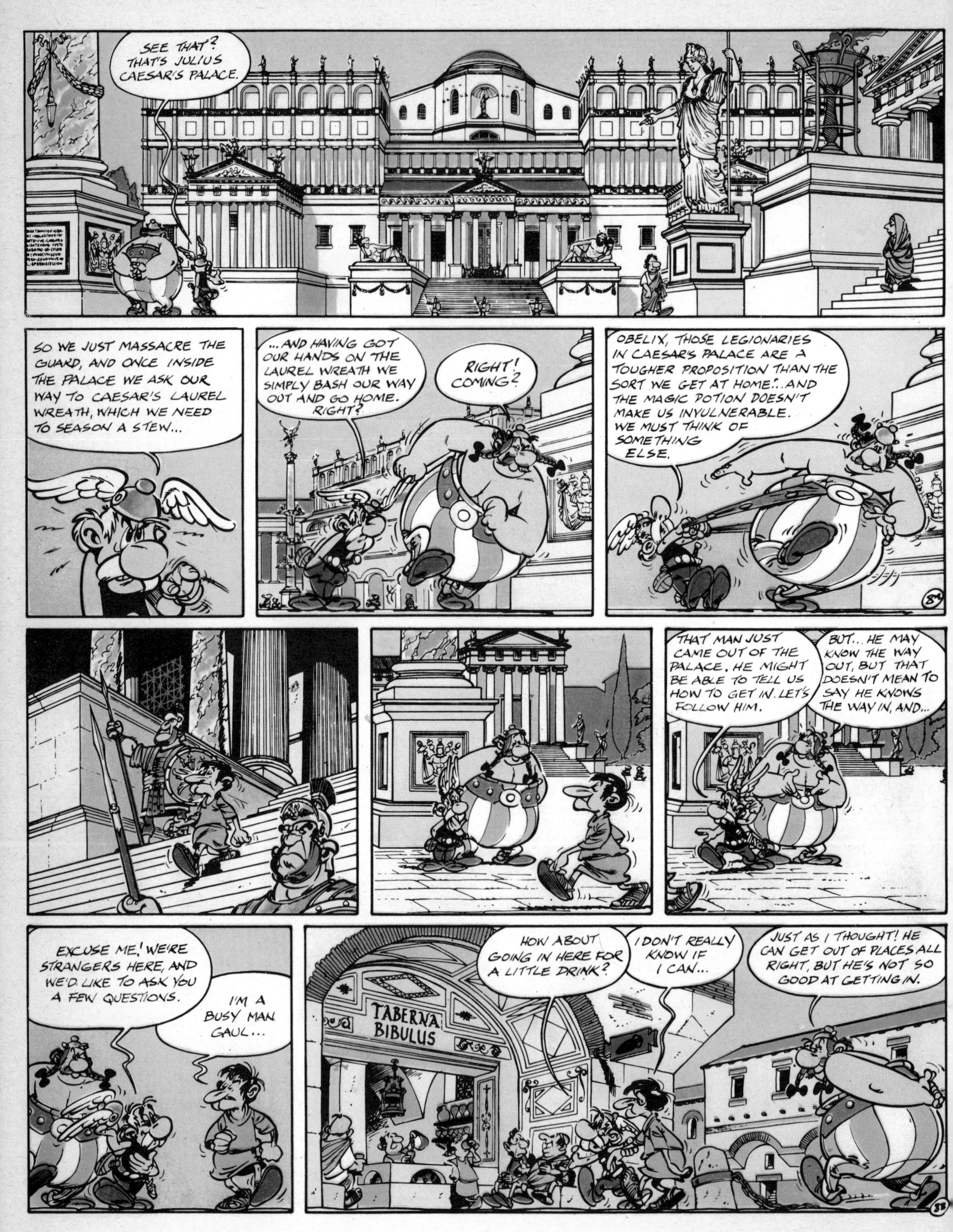
SEE THAT? THAT'S JULIUS CAESAR'S PALACE.
SO WE JUST MASSACRE THE GUARD, AND ONCE INSIDE THE PALACE WE ASK OUR WAY TO CAESAR'S LAUREL WREATH, WHICH WE NEED TO SEASON A STEW...
...AND HAVING GOT OUR HANDS ON THE LAUREL WREATH WE SIMPLY BASH OUR WAY OUT AND GO HOME. RIGHT?
RIGHT! COMING?
OBELIX, THOSE LEGIONARIES IN CAESAR'S PALACE ARE A TOUGHER PROPOSITION THAN THE SORT WE GET AT HOME... AND THE MAGIC POTION DOESN'T MAKE US INVULNERABLE. WE MUST THINK OF SOMETHING ELSE.
THAT MAN JUST CAME OUT OF THE PALACE. HE MIGHT BE ABLE TO TELL US HOW TO GET IN. LET'S FOLLOW HIM.
BUT... HE MAY KNOW THE WAY OUT, BUT THAT DOESN'T MEAN TO SAY HE KNOWS THE WAY IN, AND...
EXCUSE ME! WE'RE STRANGERS HERE, AND WE'D LIKE TO ASK YOU A FEW QUESTIONS.
I'M A BUSY MAN GAUL...
TABERNA BIBULUS
HOW ABOUT GOING IN HERE FOR A LITTLE DRINK?
I DON'T REALLY KNOW IF I CAN...
JUST AS I THOUGHT! HE CAN GET OUT OF PLACES ALL RIGHT, BUT HE'S NOT SO GOOD AT GETTING IN.

WHAT DO YOU THINK WE OUGHT TO SEE IN ROME?
OH, THERE ARE SOME INTERESTING PLACES TO VISIT! ROME, YOU KNOW, IS THE GREATEST CITY IN THE UNIVERSE.
CAESAR'S PALACE, FOR INSTANCE... COULD WE SEE OVER CAESAR'S PALACE?
DEAR ME, NO! QUITE OUT OF THE QUESTION!
BUT YOU JUST CAME OUT OF...
OH, THAT'S DIFFERENT! I AM ONE OF CAESAR'S SLAVES. MY NAME IS KUMAKROS. I WORK IN THE PALACE KITCHENS.
YOU KNOW ALL ABOUT THE STEWS THEN!
OBELIX! DRINK UP AND SHUT UP!
STEWS?
NEVER MIND HIM... HOW DOES ONE RISE TO BE CAESAR'S SLAVE?
WELL, CAESAR USUALLY GETS HIS SLAVES FROM THE HOUSE OF TYPHUS. TYPHUS IS A LUXURY-SLAVE MERCHANT HE SELLS NOTHING BUT THE BEST... IMPORTS ONLY...
TAKE ME! I'M FROM GREECE. TOP QUALITY, BUT I COST A PRETTY SESTERTIUS, I CAN TELL YOU...
THE HOUSE OF TYPHUS...
WELL, I WOULDN'T LIKE YOU TO THINK YOU WERE BORING ME, BUT I REALLY DO HAVE TO WORK LIKE A SLAVE! I HOPE YOU HAVE A NICE TIME IN ROME, GAULS. AVE.
GOODBYE.
I THINK I HAVE AN IDEA TO GET US INTO CAESAR'S PALACE... WHERE, WITH A BIT OF LUCK, WE'LL BE ABLE TO LAY HANDS ON HIS LAUREL WREATH...
ZIGACKLY!
POC!

LOOK! THAT MAN SHOULD BE ABLE TO DIRECT US.
WHAT MAKES YOU THINK SO?
THE SLAVE MARKET? I'VE JUST LEFT IT. IT'S THAT WAY.
SLAVES! SLAVES! FINE UPSTANDING SLAVES!
WHO'LL BUY MY GOTHS? NICE FRESH GOTHS!
NUUUMIDIANS! NUUUMIDIANS!
HEAVY-DUTY NIMBLE HOPLITES!
BELGIANS! BELGIANS! BELGIANS! BELGIANS!
YOU'LL NEVER WANT TO GET SHOT OF MY PARTHIANS!
DANCING-GIRLS! DANCING-GIRLS! THIS WAY FOR THE DANCING-GIRLS!
AH! THIS MUST BE IT.
THE HOUSE OF TYPHVS
BY APPOINTMENT TO JULIUS CAESAR
ARE YOU INTERESTED IN OUR WARES? WOULD YOU LIKE TO SEE THE CATALOGUE?
ARE YOU TYPHUS?
NO, THAT'S ME.
WHAT CAN I DO FOR YOU? WE'VE JUST HAD A DELIVERY OF REALLY TOP QUALITY BRITONS...

WE DON'T WANT TO BUY, WE WANT TO SELL.
SELL! OH, THAT'S DIFFERENT...
IF YOU'RE IN THE TRADE I CAN ONLY SEE YOU FIRST THING IN THE MORNING... WELL, AND WHO DID YOU HAVE TO OFFER ME?
US.
YOU? I DON'T GO BUYING ANY OLD THING.
WE'RE NOT ANY OLD THING!
THIS ONE SMELLS OF WINE.
WELL, YES, BUT HE ONLY INDULGES ONCE IN A WHILE... AND HE'S VERY STRONG.
SNIFF
SNIFF
SHOW US HOW STRONG YOU ARE OBELIX!
RIGHT.
PAF!
YES, YES... BUT I SPECIALIZE IN ELEGANT STUFF I'M EXPECTING THE PALACE MAJOR-DOMO ANY MINUTE, LET ME TELL YOU. HE'S COMING TO BUY SOME SLAVES...
SCHLONK!
I'M VERY STRONG TOO. WANT ME TO SHOW YOU?
NO! NO! DON'T BOTHER... MAFTER, I'M FURE THEY WON'T FPOIL THE DIFPLAY...
RIGHT, I'LL TAKE YOU, BUT ONLY ON SALE OR RETURN. IF I DON'T SELL YOU TODAY, YOU CAN GO AND GET SOLD SOMEWHERE ELSE.

THE HOUSE OF TYPHUS
BY APPOINTMENT TO JULIUS CAESAR
COME ON! UP ON THE PLATFORM! LET'S SEE A BIT OF CLASS! WE'RE NOT FLOGGING ANY CHEAP MASS-PRODUCED SLAVES HERE, YOU KNOW!
HMPH... I CAN SMELL THE FUMES OF WINE!
WHERE? WHERE?
PAY NO ATTENTION, MY DEAR. IT MUST BE REMNANT DAY... ONLY AN ADVERTISING GIMMICK. JUST JUNK!
JUNK? WHO'S JUNK?
YOU ARE, YOU SECOND-HAND PIECE OF GOODS!
FLAWED, AT THAT.
SHUT UP OBELIX!
YOU'LL BE FLOORED TOO IF YOU'RE NOT CAREFUL!
SHUT UP, YOU FREE GIFT!
SCHLAFF!
WHERE DO YOU THINK YOU ARE? DON'T DISTURB THE DISPLAY!
YOU SAW THAT? MY FRIEND HERE IS STRONG TOO!
I SAY, SO HE IS, OLD BOY! JOLLY GOOD SHOW!
YOU SHUT UP, BRITON, OR I'LL SELL YOU AT A DISCOUNT!
AND YOU GET OUT, GAULS!
YOU MAY FIND A DEPARTMENT STORE OR SUPERMARKET TO TAKE YOU. YOU'RE FREE!
OH NO, WE'RE NOT! AND IF NECESSARY WE'LL FIGHT TO LOSE OUR FREEDOM!
GET THESE GOODS OUT OF HERE! I'M EXPECTING CAESAR'S MAJOR-DOMO ANY MINUTE.

SUCH GOINGS-ON ARE MOST DEGRADING! I PROTEST, IN THE NAME OF THE ENTIRE STOCK!
TCHONC!
TCHAC!
HOW MUCH FOR THOSE TWO GAULS?
?
YOU... YOU WANT TO BUY THEM?
I THINK THEY'RE QUITE AMUSING.
PAF!
OF COURSE HE WANTS TO BUY US! AND HE'LL BE MAKING A GOOD DEAL, WON'T HE, OBELIX?
QUITE RIGHT! WE'RE A GOOD DEAL OF A GOOD DEAL, TOO!
THAT DEPENDS HOW MUCH DO YOU COST?
NAME YOUR PRICE! HE'LL TAKE IT.
NO, GO ON, DO! YOU NAME A PRICE.
FIVE SESTERTII THE PAIR, ALL RIGHT?
OH, COME NOW! WAIT A MINUTE...
OH, I SAY! THIS IS RIDICULOUS, EH, WHAT? SELLING AT A PRICE LIKE THAT WILL DEVALUE THE WHOLE STOCK!
HOW ABOUT SIX THEN?
MAY I GET A WORD IN EDGEWAYS?
TEN! BRITONS NEVER, NEVER, NEVER SHALL BE CUT-PRICE SLAVES!
VS
JULIUS CAES
DONE!
HERE YOU ARE!
OH, NO! ALLOW ME!
WELL, IF YOU INSIST. I'LL DO AS MUCH FOR YOU ONE OF THESE DAYS

FOLLOW ME.
THE HOUSE OF TYPHUS
ONCE INSIDE CAESAR'S PALACE, WE'LL SET ABOUT LOOKING FOR HIS LAURELS!
SO LONG AS HE ISN'T RESTING ON THEM!
SOON AFTERWARDS...
HERE WE ARE.
HEY, ASTERIX... THIS ISN'T CAESAR'S PALACE, IS IT?
PERHAPS HE HAS SEVERAL...
FIBULA! TIBIA! NITWIT! COME AND LOOK AT THIS!
SEE THESE GAULS? I GOT THEM FROM THE HOUSE OF TYPHUS.
THE HOUSE OF TYPHUS? YOU MUST BE MAD, OSSEUS! HE'S TERRIBLY EXPENSIVE.
AND WHEN I THINK OF THE FUSS THEY KICK UP IN THIS DOMUS WHEN I WANT TO BUY A NEW TOGA!
IS THAT WHAT ALL THE SHOUTING WAS ABOUT?
I THOUGHT IT WOULD BE A NICE SURPRISE.. THEY'RE RATHER AMUSING.
OH WELL, I'M GOING BACK TO MY CUBICULUM TO GET A BIT OF SLEEP.
YOU'VE BEEN OUT DRINKING ALL NIGHT WITH YOUR FRIENDS AGAIN! YOU'LL FIND YOURSELF IN MY LIBRI NIGRI* IF YOU DON'T WATCH OUT!
I SAY... ISN'T THIS CAESAR'S PALACE?
* BLACK BOOKS
CAESAR'S PALACE?
YOU'RE RIGHT, THEY ARE AMUSING!

WHY, NO, GAUL! THIS ISN'T CAESAR'S PALACE! THIS HOUSE BELONGS TO ME, OSSEUS HUMERUS...
AND THIS IS MY WIFE FIBULA, MY DAUGHTER TIBIA, AND MY NITWIT OF A SON, METATARSUS.
??
BUT WHAT ARE WE GOING TO DO WITH THEM? WE HAVE ALL THE SLAVES WE NEED.
THEY COULD WORK IN THE KITCHEN. GAULISH CUISINE IS GOOD... ANYWAY, IT CAN'T BE ANY WORSE THAN WHAT OUR BRITISH SLAVE AUTODIDAX GIVES US.
GOLDEN-DELICIUS!
YES, MASTER?
GOLDENDELICIUS, TAKE THESE TWO GAULISH SLAVES TO THE KITCHEN. THEY ARE TO PREPARE OUR MEALS.
GO WITH OUR MAJOR-DOMO, GOLDENDELICIUS.
LOOK HERE...
AND TAKE CARE OF THEM. THEY'RE FROM THE HOUSE OF TYPHUS!
WELL, THIS IS ALL YOURS, YOU TWO PRECIOUS WORKS OF ART!
TWO WHAT?
WORKS OF ART! I'M NOT A WORK OF ART FROM THE HOUSE OF TYPHUS, NOT ME! I'M NOT FRAGILE LIKE YOU, BUT THIS IS A GOOD JOB I'VE GOT HERE, EVEN IF IT IS IN A MADHOUSE...
AND DON'T YOU GO TRYING TO EDGE ME OUT OF IT!
SLAM!
THAT ROMAN IS CRAZY! THIS IS THE FIRST TIME ANYONE EVER TOLD ME I WAS FRAGILE!
TOC! TOC! TOC! TOC!

WE'VE MADE A MISTAKE... ALL THIS IS ONLY TAKING US FURTHER AWAY FROM CAESAR'S LAUREL WREATH.
WELL THEN, LET'S GO.
NO. WE'RE SLAVES. IF WE RUN AWAY WE'LL NEVER HAVE A CHANCE OF GETTING INTO CAESAR'S PALACE.
WE MUST PERSUADE HUMERUS TO RETURN US TO TYPHUS TO BE RESOLD.
JUST LIKE THE PEOPLE WHO BUY YOUR MENHIRS AND BRING THEM BACK. BECAUSE THEY'RE NOT SATISFIED.
ALL MY CUSTOMERS ARE SATISFIED!
AH, BUT YOUR MENHIRS DON'T DO THE COOKING...
WE'LL MAKE THEM A MEAL THEY WON'T FORGET IN A HURRY, BY TOUTATIS! BRING ME EVERYTHING YOU CAN FIND IN THE LARDER!
HERE YOU ARE! JAM, BLACK PEPPERCORNS, SALT, KIDNEYS, CARBOLIX SOAP, A CHICKEN, HONEY, RED PEPPERS, BLACK PUDDING, EGGS, AND POMEGRANATE SEEDS!
I'VE FOUND SOME MORE RED PEPPERS AND BLACK PEPPERCORNS... WE'LL FLING IT ALL IN THE POT!
HOW ABOUT THE CHICKEN? SHALL I PLUCK IT?
WHY BOTHER?
SOON AFTERWARDS...
IT'S NEARLY DONE.
CAN I HAVE A TASTE?

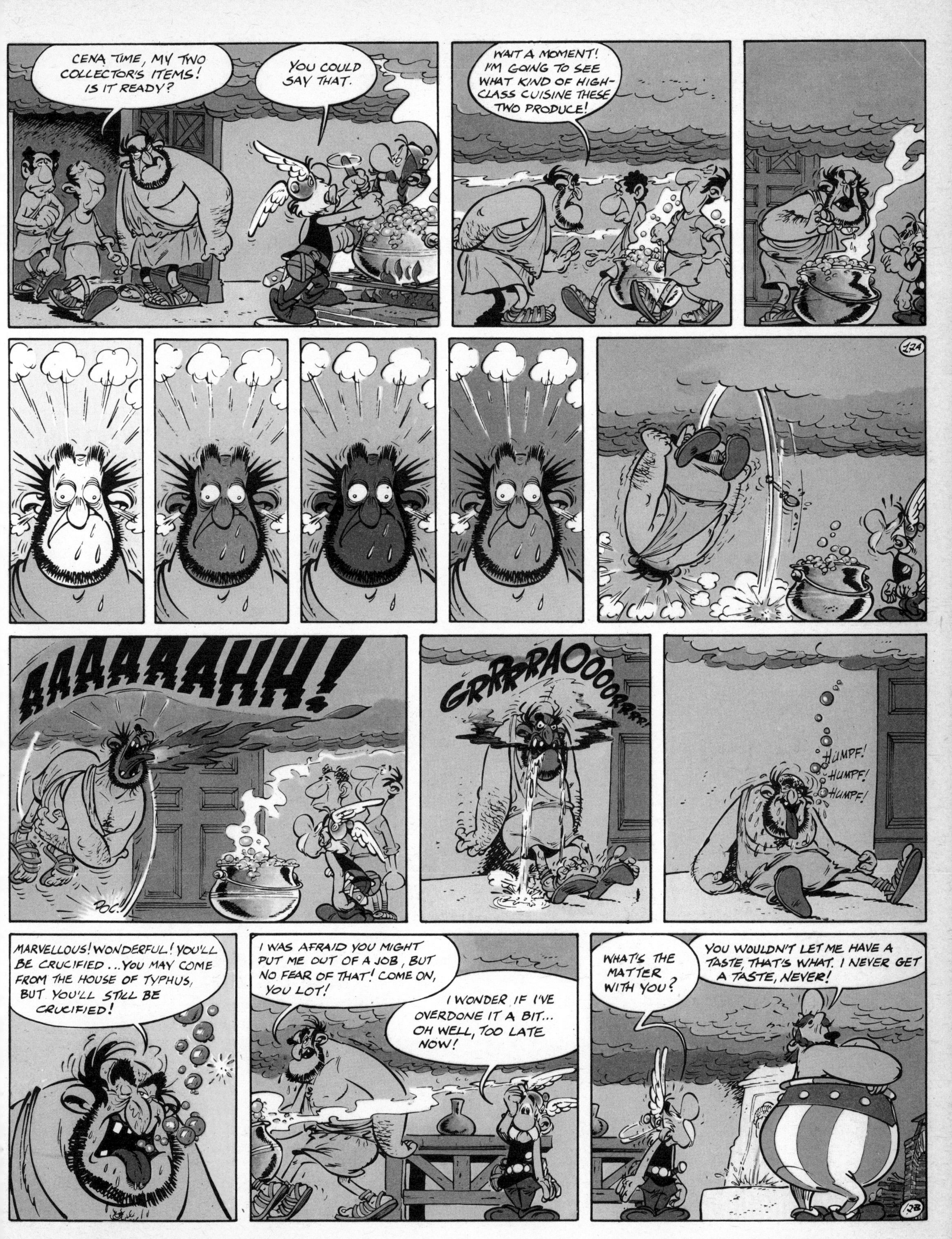
CENA TIME, MY TWO COLLECTOR'S ITEMS! IS IT READY?
YOU COULD SAY THAT.
WAIT A MOMENT! I'M GOING TO SEE WHAT KIND OF HIGH-CLASS CUISINE THESE TWO PRODUCE!
AAAAAAHH!
POC!
GRRRRAOOOORRRR!
HUMPF! HUMPF! HUMPF!
MARVELLOUS! WONDERFUL! YOU'LL BE CRUCIFIED...YOU MAY COME FROM THE HOUSE OF TYPHUS, BUT YOU'LL STILL BE CRUCIFIED!
I WAS AFRAID YOU MIGHT PUT ME OUT OF A JOB, BUT NO FEAR OF THAT! COME ON, YOU LOT!
I WONDER IF I'VE OVERDONE IT A BIT... OH WELL, TOO LATE NOW!
WHAT'S THE MATTER WITH YOU?
YOU WOULDN'T LET ME HAVE A TASTE, THAT'S WHAT. I NEVER GET A TASTE, NEVER!

METATARSUS! GET OUT OF YOUR CUBICULUM AND COME INTO THE TRICLINIUM! CENA IS SERVED!
LOOK, I'LL DO ANYTHING, ANYTHING, ONLY DON'T SHOUT LIKE THAT... I'D FEEL BETTER FLAT ON MY CUBILE, BUT IF...
THE FACT THAT YOU HAVE MANAGED TO DECUBILATE YOURSELF GIVES YOU NO RIGHT TO BEHAVE BADLY. LIE DOWN TO THE TABLE PROPERLY.
IT DOES SMELL FUNNY...
NOT FOR ME, THANKS.
THIS MEAL WAS COOKED BY MY TWO GAULS FROM THE HOUSE OF TYPHUS! YOU'LL EAT IT AND LIKE IT!!!
GLOP!
etc...
TEEHEE HEE!
SCRUNCH! SCRUNCH!
WHERE ARE THEY? WHERE ARE THEY?
OBELIX, I RATHER THINK THE MOMENT HAS COME TO SELL OUR LIVES DEARLY!
DIDN'T WE SELL THEM BEFORE?

?
COME TO MY ARMS!
!?
YOUR MIRACULOUS DISH HAS CURED ME LIKE A SHOT!
THANKS TO YOU TWO, I'LL BE ABLE TO SPEND THE NIGHT DRINKING AND MAKING MERRY WITH MY FRIENDS, HAPPY IN THE KNOWLEDGE THAT NEXT DAY YOU WILL COOK UP THIS EXCELLENT CONCOCTION TO MAKE A NEW MAN OF ME!
COME ON! COME ON! THE FAMILY WANTS TO CONGRATULATE YOU!
HEY, PATER, PATER! WE DON'T OFTEN SEE OCULUS TO OCULUS, BUT YOU REALLY WERE INSPIRED WHEN YOU BOUGHT THESE TWO THEY'RE MARVELS!
WHAT A WONDERFUL RECIPE!
GLAD YOU LIKED IT, MY BOY... YES, EXCELLENT, BUT IT IS A BIT STRONG... WE WON'T ASK THE GAULS TO DO ANY MORE COOKING EXCEPT ON SPECIAL OCCASIONS. AND NOW LET'S GO TO BED...
I DON'T UNDERSTAND... HOW CAN THEY HAVE LIKED IT?
YOU'RE RIGHT...
IT WAS A BIT INSIPID.
?!

YOU MAY HAVE GOT AWAY UNCRUCIFIED, BUT I'LL HAVE YOU THROWN TO THE LIONS YET... THEY DON'T OFTEN TASTE CHOICE TITBITS FROM THE HOUSE OF TYPHUS, POOR THINGS!
MEANWHILE, SLEEP TIGHT, MY WORKS OF ART! WE RISE AT DAWN IN THIS HOUSE, AND I SHALL KEEP YOUR NOSES TO THE GRINDSTONE!
ASTERIX, DO YOU THINK WE'LL END UP AS CHOICE TITBITS FED TO THE LIONS?
I DON'T KNOW ABOUT THAT, OBELIX, BUT I HAVE AN IDEA THAT WILL MAKE THE ROMANS FED UP WITH US!
WE'LL KEEP THEM AWAKE ALL NIGHT... AND SINCE THE ROMANS RISE AT DAWN, THEY WON'T LIKE THAT.
WE'LL BE SOLD BACK FIRST THING TOMORROW.
IT'S TIME!
HGMFFF-FKHGPFFF!
WE NEED SOMETHING TO MAKE A LOUD NOISE. LET'S TRY THE KITCHEN.
COULDN'T WE MAKE A LOUD NOISE BY SNORING?
BLOING! CLANG!
BLOMM!
BLOIM!
CLANG!

CLANG! BLOIMM! CLANG! BLOIMM! CLANG!
WHAT'S GOING ON?
THE BARBARIANS! IT'S THE FALL OF THE ROMAN EMPIRE!
BLOIMM! CLANG! BLOIMM! CLANG! CLANG! CLANG!
WHAT ARE YOU DOING, BY JUPITER?
WE JUST CAN'T HELP IT, WE GAULS, IT'S IN OUR BLOOD! WE HAVE TO MAKE MERRY AT NIGHT!
BLOIMM! CLANG
MASTER, WOULD YOU LIKE ME TO HAVE THEM WHIPPED?
WHIP SLAVES FROM THE HOUSE OF TYPHUS? DO YOU THINK GAULS GROW ON TREES?
CLANG! BLOIMM!
WHAT'S ALL THIS? EVERYONE AWAKE?
IS THIS THE SORT OF HOUR YOU CHOOSE TO COME HOME, YOU DISSOLUTE BOY?
JUST IN TIME, TOO! I SEE YOU'RE HAVING SOME FUN IN THIS DOMUS FOR ONCE!
CLANG
OH YES! LET'S HAVE FUN, LIKE THE GAULS!
I'M GOING TO FIND MY FRIENDS! THEY CAN'T HAVE GOT FAR, NOT IN THE STATE THEY'RE IN!
BUT...
CLANG!
OH YES, OSSEUS DARLING! LET'S HAVE A SURPRISE ORGY, LIKE WHEN WE WERE YOUNG!
CLANG! CLANG! CL...
?!?
GOLDENDELICIUS! LIGHT THE LAMPS! FETCH SOME WINE! SEND FOR MUSICIANS AND BRING ON THE DANCING-GIRLS!
SOON AFTERWARDS...
CLANG! TZIIING! BLING! HAHAHA HIHIHI!
I SAY, ASTERIX, DO YOU THINK WE COULD RESELL THESE ROMANS?

THE SUN RISES UPON A HOUSE WHICH HAS FINALLY FALLEN SILENT...
COME ON, YOU LOT! BRING OUT YOUR MAPPAE AND SCOPAE! *
* FLOORCLOTHS AND BROOMS
CLEAN THE PLACE UP! I'M GOING TO WAKE THE MASTER.
22A
MASTER, THE SUN IS ALREADY HIGH IN THE SKY. AM I TO SEND FOR THE TONSOR TO SHAVE YOU?
NO! AND TELL ALL THOSE OTHER IDIOTS THAT IF THEY GO ON MAKING THAT NOISE I'LL SELL THEM OFF AS A JOB LOT, WITH YOU AND THE TONSOR THROWN IN!
OOOOH! MY HEAD...
ER... MASTER... MAY I REMIND YOU THAT YOU HAVE AN IMPORTANT ENGAGEMENT AT THE PALACE THIS MORNING? AM I TO GO AND SAY YOU'RE ILL?
HMM? NO... I'LL SEND MY GAULS FROM THE HOUSE OF TYPHUS, THAT WILL LOOK MORE ELEGANT. NOW LEAVE ME ALONE. I FEEL A BIT EX COLORE. CLEAR OFF!
22B
OH, SO THEY'VE SUPPLANTED ME! SO THEY'RE GOING TO THE PALACE INSTEAD, EH? RIGHT! I HAVE AN IDEA!...

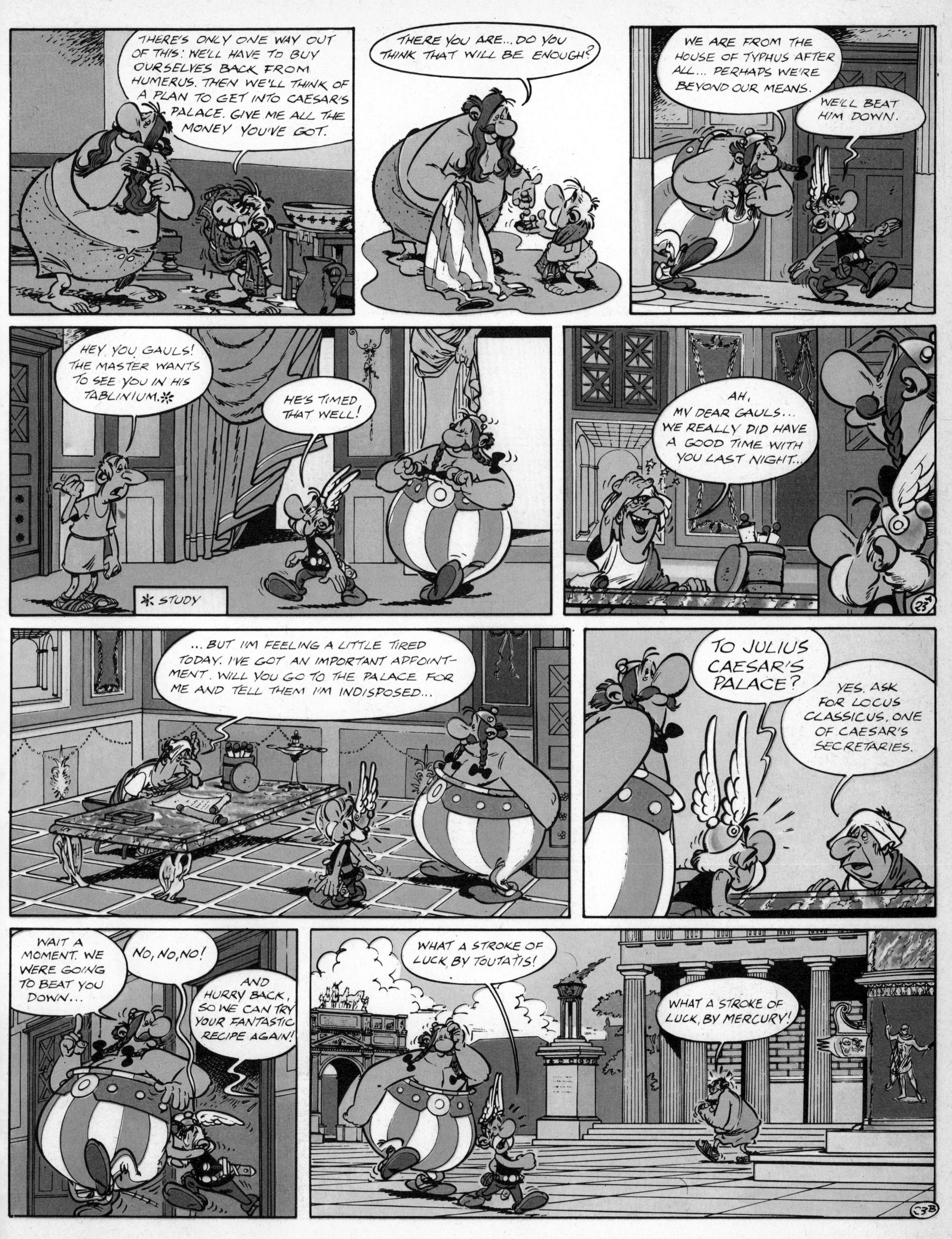
THERE'S ONLY ONE WAY OUT OF THIS: WE'LL HAVE TO BUY OURSELVES BACK FROM HUMERUS. THEN WE'LL THINK OF A PLAN TO GET INTO CAESAR'S PALACE. GIVE ME ALL THE MONEY YOU'VE GOT.
THERE YOU ARE... DO YOU THINK THAT WILL BE ENOUGH?
WE ARE FROM THE HOUSE OF TYPHUS AFTER ALL... PERHAPS WE'RE BEYOND OUR MEANS.
WE'LL BEAT HIM DOWN.
HEY, YOU GAULS! THE MASTER WANTS TO SEE YOU IN HIS TABLINIUM.*
HE'S TIMED THAT WELL!
* STUDY
AH, MY DEAR GAULS... WE REALLY DID HAVE A GOOD TIME WITH YOU LAST NIGHT...
... BUT I'M FEELING A LITTLE TIRED TODAY. I'VE GOT AN IMPORTANT APPOINTMENT. WILL YOU GO TO THE PALACE FOR ME AND TELL THEM I'M INDISPOSED...
TO JULIUS CAESAR'S PALACE?
YES. ASK FOR LOCUS CLASSICUS, ONE OF CAESAR'S SECRETARIES.
WAIT A MOMENT. WE WERE GOING TO BEAT YOU DOWN...
NO, NO, NO!
AND HURRY BACK, SO WE CAN TRY YOUR FANTASTIC RECIPE AGAIN!
WHAT A STROKE OF LUCK, BY TOUTATIS!
WHAT A STROKE OF LUCK, BY MERCURY!

NOW WHAT? HAVE WE GIVEN UP THE IDEA OF BUYING OURSELVES BACK?
WE DON'T NEED TO! WE'VE GOT A GOOD EXCUSE TO GET INTO CAESAR'S PALACE NOW!
ONCE INSIDE, WE'LL FIND A WAY TO GATHER CAESAR'S LAURELS!
WHAT A PITY! I SHOULD HAVE LIKED TO BUY US... WE WOULD HAVE MADE A NICE SOUVENIR TO TAKE HOME FROM OUR TRIP.
HALT! QUO VADIS?
WE HAVE COME ON BEHALF OF OUR MASTER, OSSEOUS HUMERUS, WITH A MESSAGE FOR...
...FOR LOCUS CLASSICUS, CAESAR'S SECRETARY. COME IN, COME IN! YOU'RE EXPECTED.
TEEHEEHEE-HEE!
?
HE LET US VADERE QUO WE WANTED TO GO VERY READILY... THIS IS EASY!
TOO EASY... HOW DOES HE KNOW WE'RE EXPECTED?
HOLD IT THERE, GAULS!!
?!?

???
RIGHT! SHALL WE GET THEM?
NO. LET'S FIND OUT WHAT THEY WANT ANYWAY. THEY COULD HACK US TO PIECES WITH THEIR WEAPONS
HUH! WE'RE OUR OWN MASTERS, AREN'T WE...?
SO YOU WANT TO ASSASSINATE JULIUS CAESAR, DO YOU?
?
AN HONEST SLAVE, WHO WILL BE REWARDED FOR HIS SERVICES, HAS DENOUNCED YOU. HE DISCOVERED YOUR PLOT
... YOU USED A TRICK TO INFILTRATE THE HOUSE OF OSSEUS HUMERUS, IN ORDER TO FIND A PRETEXT TO GET INTO CAESAR'S PALACE AND KILL HIM!
?
TAKE THEM AWAY TO THE PALACE PRISON!
THE PALACE PRISON...
WE DIDN'T WANT TO KILL OLD JULIUS, DID WE, ASTERIX?
DO YOU DENY YOU HAVE DESIGNS ON OUR HEAD OF STATE?
ONLY WHAT'S ON IT.
WHAT'S THE GOOD OF PROTESTING, OBELIX? WE'RE DONE FOR
TAKE THEM AWAY!
?

?
IN YOU GO!
I DON'T UNDERSTAND, ASTERIX! WHY ARE WE LETTING THEM TREAT US LIKE THIS? THEY'RE ONLY ROMANS, AFTER ALL!
VLAN!
BUT THIS IS WONDERFUL, OBELIX! WE'RE IN THE PALACE! TONIGHT WE CAN GET OUT OF OUR CELL AND LOOK AROUND FOR CAESAR'S LAUREL WREATH AT OUR LEISURE!
WHAT! WE DON'T GET ANY SLEEP TONIGHT EITHER?
VERITAS ODIUM PARIT
CXVII DAYS TILL I GET OUT
NO SEDITIOUS GRAFFITI
GLORIA VICTIS
DEATH TO THE LIONS
AND SO, THAT NIGHT...
OPEN THE DOOR AS QUIETLY AS POSSIBLE.
?
CLONG!
CLANG!
THEY MAKE MORE NOISE COMING DOWN THAN GOING UP
BIFF!
LET'S GO!

WE'LL SEARCH EVERYWHERE, AS QUIETLY AS POSSIBLE.
PIF! POF!
THIS GUARD'S A BIG ONE!
STILL NO SIGN OF IT. THE PALACE IS ENORMOUS, AND A LAUREL WREATH ISN'T VERY BIG.
I'LL JUST DUMP THESE HERE... WE SEEM TO BE GETTING ON TOP OF ONE ANOTHER. THEN WE CAN GO ON.
WHEN ARE WE GOING TO GET SOME SLEEP? THEY WON'T LET US LIE IN, I BET!
NO, NO. IT'S NEARLY DAYLIGHT. LET'S GET BACK TO OUR CELL. WE'LL CARRY ON TOMORROW NIGHT.

ANOTHER SUNNY DAY HAS JUST DAWNED UPON THE GREATEST CITY IN THE UNIVERSE: ROME!
SOUND THE ALARM!
THE PRISONERS HAVE ESCAPED!
WHERE AM I?
ON TOP OF ME, YOU IDIOT!
THEY KNOCKED OUT ALL THE GUARDS ON NIGHT DUTY. THIS IS REALLY GETTING ON TOP OF ME!
LOOK, CENTURION! THE LOCK IS BROKEN!
BY JUPITER!
YOU ROMANS MUST BE CRAZY! IS THERE NO WAY OF GETTING ANY SLEEP ROUND HERE???
!?!
DEATH TO THE LIONS
YOU... YOU HAVEN'T ESCAPED?
NO! SHUT THE DOOR, AND GET THAT LOCK REPAIRED!
I... I'M SORRY...
HUH! WE CAN'T GET PEACE AND QUIET ANYWHERE!
THEY'RE WIZARDS!
GAULISH DRUIDS, PERHAPS...
THE GAULS HAVE STRANGE AND TERRIBLE GODS...!
WE MUST GET RID OF THEM, AND QUICKLY! I WAS WAITING FOR CAESAR TO RETURN; HOWEVER, IT CAN'T BE HELPED... MEANWHILE, DOUBLE THE GUARD! SPREAD YOURSELVES OUT! DON'T GET ON TOP OF ONE ANOTHER!

I DON'T LIKE BIG TOWNS; I NEVER SLEEP WELL THERE. I FEEL HEMMED IN... SHUT UP...
WHAT WE MUST DO IS FIND CAESAR... HE'S GENERALLY TO BE FOUND JUST UNDERNEATH HIS LAUREL WREATH.
AH! SO THESE ARE MY CLIENTS!
YOUR CLIENTS?
YES, I'M YOUR LAWYER, TITUS NISIPRIUS.
YOU ARE GOING TO BE TRIED THIS VERY DAY, AND I'VE BEEN ASSIGNED TO YOU AS LEGAL AID. IT'S A GOOD BRIEF FOR ME. TWO GAULISH WIZARDS— THAT'LL ATTRACT A LARGE CROWD!
I HAVE A VERY FINE SPEECH PREPARED. IT BEGINS LIKE THIS: DELENDA CARTHAGO, SAID THE GREAT CATO...
ARE YOU GOING TO GET US SET FREE?
YOU MUST BE JOKING! LOTS OF WILD ANIMALS HAVE ARRIVED IN THE CIRCUS, AND THEY'VE HAD NOTHING SUBSTANTIAL TO GET THEIR TEETH INTO... SO YOU SEE, TWO GAULISH WIZARDS, JUST THINK! WHAT A SHOW!
DOES JULIUS CAESAR GO TO THESE SHOWS?
USUALLY, YES... DELENDA CARTHAGO, I SHALL SAY TO THEM...
AND WHEN HE GOES TO THE CIRCUS, DOES HE WEAR HIS LAUREL WREATH?
I'VE NEVER SEEN HIM IN A STRAW HAT, MY FRIEND... WHY DON'T YOU LISTEN TO MY PLEA FOR THE DEFENCE? DELENDA CARTHAGO SAID THE GREAT CATO...
?
BONG! BONG!
BRING THE GAULISH WIZARDS BEFORE THE COURT!

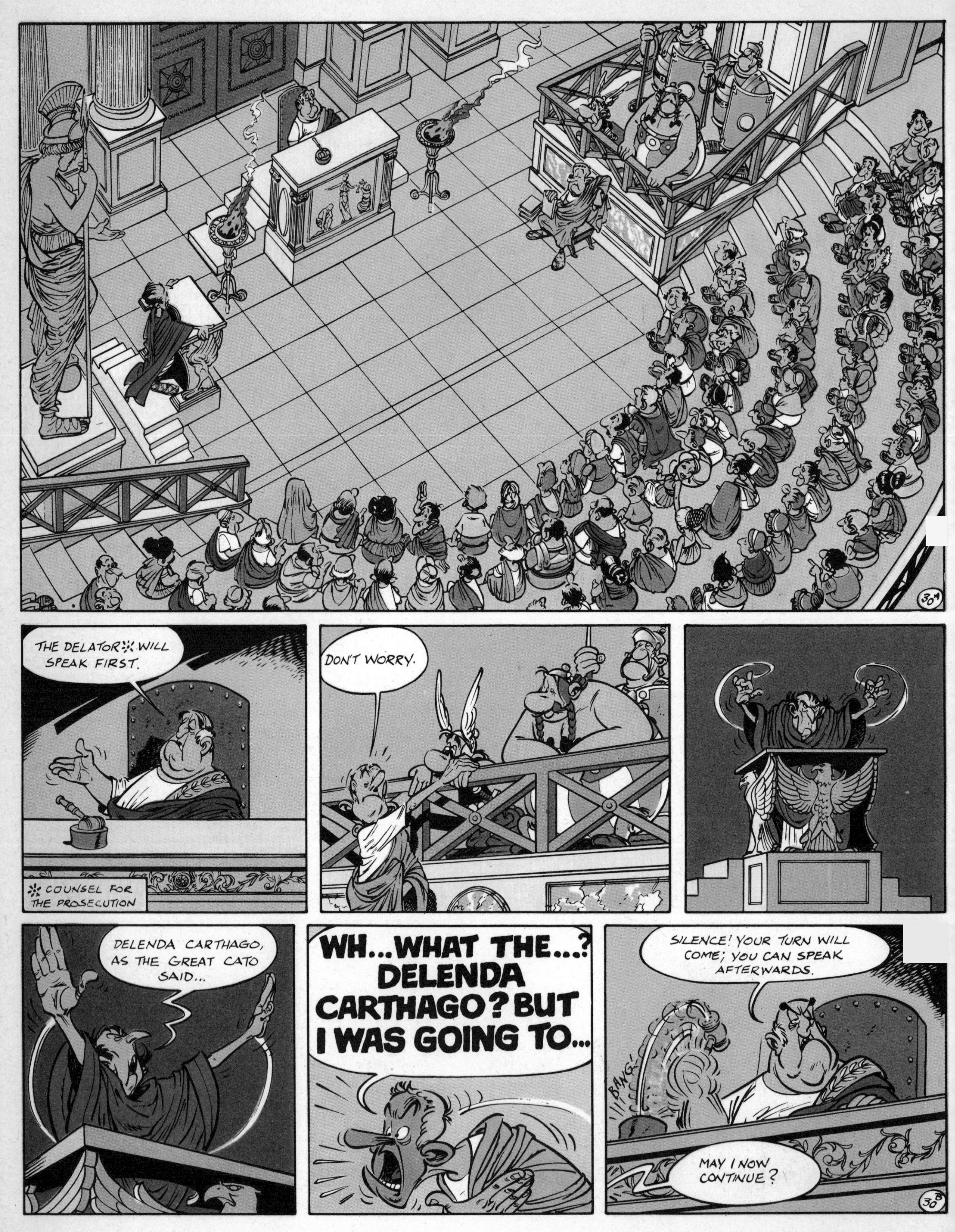
THE DELATOR* WILL SPEAK FIRST.
* COUNSEL FOR THE PROSECUTION
DON'T WORRY.
DELENDA CARTHAGO, AS THE GREAT CATO SAID...
WH...WHAT THE...? DELENDA CARTHAGO? BUT I WAS GOING TO...
SILENCE! YOUR TURN WILL COME; YOU CAN SPEAK AFTERWARDS.
BANG!
MAY I NOW CONTINUE?

YOU MAY SPEAK, DELATOR.
SO IT IS CATO YOU HEAR, SPEAKING THROUGH ME... DELENDA CARTHAGO, AS I WAS SAYING, AND...
I WOULD REQUEST AN ADJOURNMENT IN ORDER TO RECONSIDER MY DEFENCE.
RHUBARBRHUBARBRHUBARBRHUBARBRHUBARBRHUBARBRHUBARBRHUBARBRH
SILENCE IN COURT! DELATOR, HAVE YOU ANY OBJECTIONS TO THE DEFENCE COUNSEL'S REQUEST?
NONE WHATSOEVER.
BANG! BANG! BANG!
WELL, I HAVE BY TOUTATIS!
RHUBARBRHUBARBRHUBARBRHUBARBRHUBAR
BANG! BANG! BANG! BANG!
SILENCE! SILENCE, OR I'LL HAVE THE COURT CLEARED!
AND WHAT ABOUT THE WILD ANIMALS? THE POOR THINGS MUST BE FED. UNHAPPY CREATURES, THEY KNOW NOTHING OF THE COURSE OF HUMAN JUSTICE...!
WILL YOU ALLOW THIS? YOU SEE BEFORE YOU TWO FOREIGNERS OF DOUBTFUL REPUTATION...
... WHO HAVE ABUSED THE GOOD FAITH OF AN HONEST AND REPUTABLE SLAVE DEALER...!

TWO FOREIGNERS WHO HAVE DECEITFULLY INFILTRATED A FAMILY HIGHLY RESPECTED IN THE CITY, WITH THE SOLE AIM OF FINDING A PRETEXT FOR A COWARDLY ATTEMPT ON THE LIFE OF THE ILLUSTRIOUS PERSON OF JULIUS CAESAR...
... AND YOU WASTE YOUR TIME IN FUTILE ARGUMENTS? IN ENDLESS SPEECHES?
I SAY NOOOO! JUDGES, I SAY NO! THROW THEM TO THE LIONS! TO THE LIONS, I SAY!
AND MAY CAESAR HIMSELF, WEARING THE LAUREL WREATH HE SO RICHLY DESERVES, WITNESS THE FEASTING OF THESE HARMLESS ANIMALS...
... WHOSE FANGS WILL THUS BECOME THE MIGHTY SWORD OF IMPERIAL JUSTICE... THAT IS THE CASE FOR THE PROSECUTION.
SNIFF! SNIFF! SNIFF! SNIFF! SNIFF! SNIFF! SNIFF! SNIFF! SNIFF! SNIFF!
SNIF!
I-I FIND THE ACCUSED GUILTY. I SENTENCE THEM TO BE THROWN TO THE LIONS IN THE CIRCUS MAXIMUS!
BRAVO! BRAVO! HEAR, HEAR!
BANG!
LONG LIVE THE PRISONERS! BRAVO!
BRAVO! HEAR, HEAR!
CLEAR THE COURT! LEGIONARIES, CLEAR THE COURT!
NOT EXACTLY A CLASSIC SUMMING-UP BUT SO MOVING!
THOSE WILD ANIMALS ARE LUCKY! VERY, VERY LUCKY!

ONE OF THE SINISTER CELLS IN THE CIRCUS MAXIMUS...
TYPHUS HAS SENT YOU THIS AMPHORA OF WINE, AND THESE DELICACIES ARE FROM THE HUMERUS FAMILY...
THAT ROAST BOAR WAS GOOD.
THAT'S THE ADVANTAGE OF BEING THROWN TO THE LIONS. YOU ALWAYS GET TASTY GOURMET DISHES...
WHEREAS THOSE THROWN FROM THE TARPEIAN ROCK GET SOLID, HEAVY FOOD.
THERE'S A FANTASTIC LINE-UP ON THE PROGRAMME: LIONS, PANTHERS, LEOPARDS, TIGERS! ALL FINE SPECIMENS! THEY'VE EATEN NOTHING BUT LETTUCE FOR A WHOLE WEEK NOW!
SO YOU HAVE NO CAUSE FOR COMPLAINT! YOU REALLY ARE SPOILT!
CLANG!
ASTERIX, I'M SCARED.
SCARED? SCARED OF A FEW WILD ANIMALS?
OH, I'M NOT WORRIED ABOUT THE ANIMALS, IT'S THE PUBLIC! ALL THOSE PEOPLE!
YOU'LL BE ALL RIGHT IN THE ARENA...
I'M SURE THAT ONCE THE SHOW BEGINS OTHER PRISONERS FORGET THEIR STAGE FRIGHT TOO AND THINK OF NOTHING BUT THE ANIMALS.
I'M AFRAID OF LETTING THE... AUDIENCE DOWN... LOOKING SILLY...
EXCUSE ME, YOU WOULDN'T HAVE A DROP OF OIL TO RUB ME DOWN WITH, WOULD YOU - LIKE THE GLADIATORS? IT LOOKS GOOD.
OIL?
DON'T YOU THINK MUSTARD WOULD BE MORE APPROPRIATE.

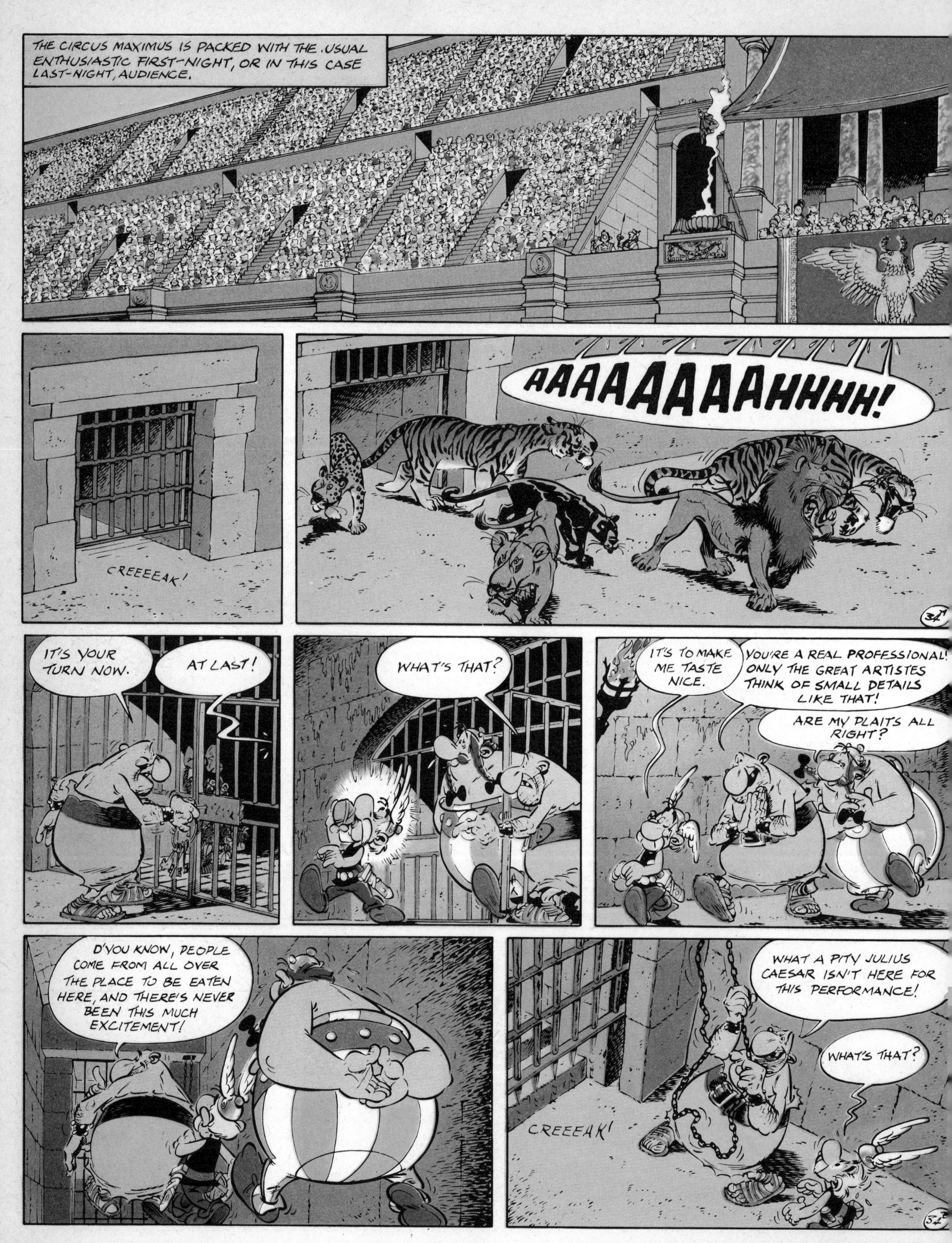
THE CIRCUS MAXIMUS IS PACKED WITH THE USUAL ENTHUSIASTIC FIRST-NIGHT, OR IN THIS CASE LAST-NIGHT, AUDIENCE.
CREEEEAK!
AAAAAAAAAHHHH!
IT'S YOUR TURN NOW.
AT LAST!
WHAT'S THAT?
IT'S TO MAKE ME TASTE NICE.
YOU'RE A REAL PROFESSIONAL! ONLY THE GREAT ARTISTES THINK OF SMALL DETAILS LIKE THAT!
ARE MY PLAITS ALL RIGHT?
D'YOU KNOW, PEOPLE COME FROM ALL OVER THE PLACE TO BE EATEN HERE, AND THERE'S NEVER BEEN THIS MUCH EXCITEMENT!
WHAT A PITY JULIUS CAESAR ISN'T HERE FOR THIS PERFORMANCE!
WHAT'S THAT?
CREEEAK!

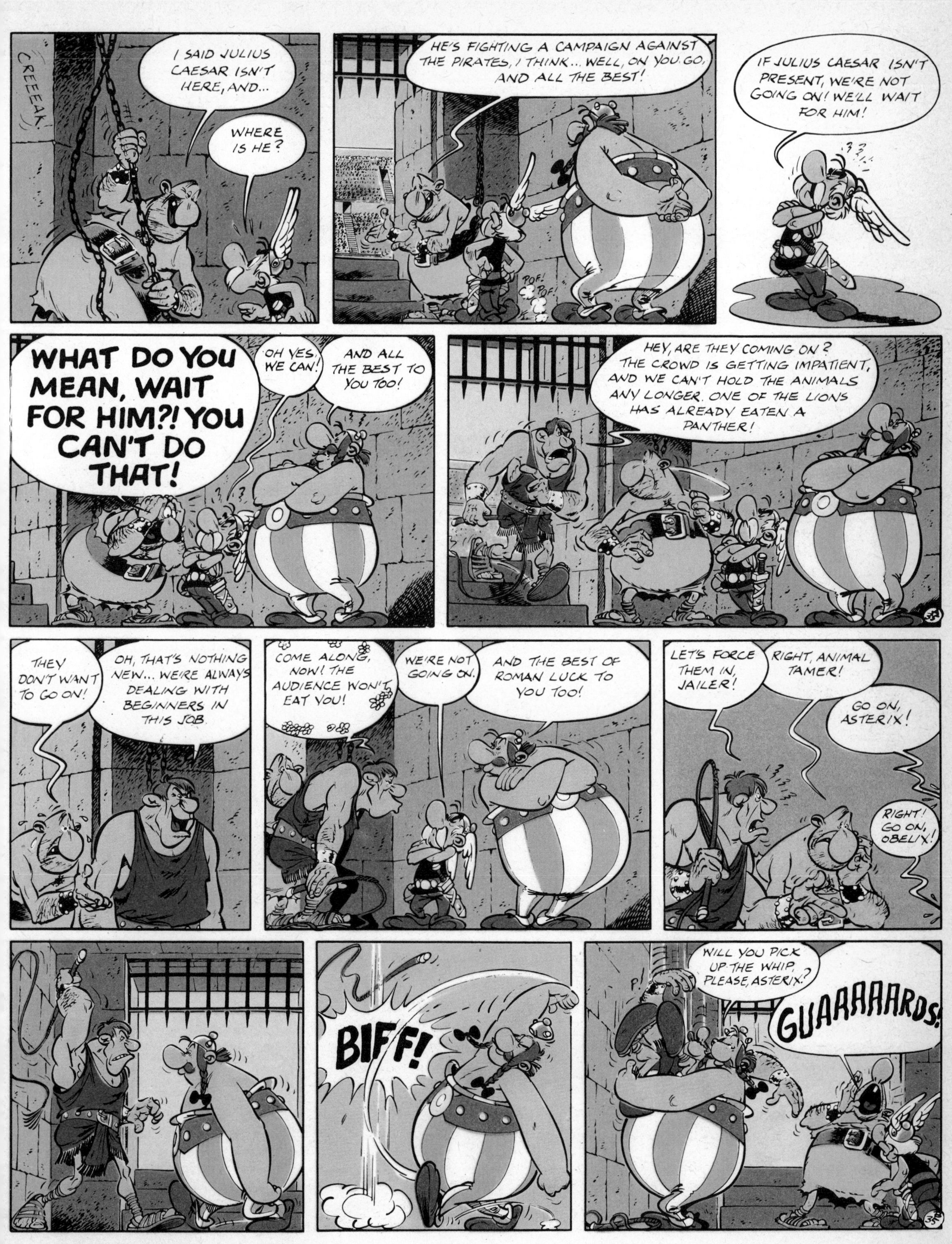
CREEEAK
I SAID JULIUS CAESAR ISN'T HERE, AND...
WHERE IS HE?
HE'S FIGHTING A CAMPAIGN AGAINST THE PIRATES, I THINK... WELL, ON YOU GO, AND ALL THE BEST!
POF! POF!
IF JULIUS CAESAR ISN'T PRESENT, WE'RE NOT GOING ON! WE'LL WAIT FOR HIM!
WHAT DO YOU MEAN, WAIT FOR HIM?! YOU CAN'T DO THAT!
OH YES, WE CAN!
AND ALL THE BEST TO YOU TOO!
HEY, ARE THEY COMING ON? THE CROWD IS GETTING IMPATIENT, AND WE CAN'T HOLD THE ANIMALS ANY LONGER. ONE OF THE LIONS HAS ALREADY EATEN A PANTHER!
THEY DON'T WANT TO GO ON!
OH, THAT'S NOTHING NEW... WE'RE ALWAYS DEALING WITH BEGINNERS IN THIS JOB.
COME ALONG, NOW! THE AUDIENCE WON'T EAT YOU!
WE'RE NOT GOING ON.
AND THE BEST OF ROMAN LUCK TO YOU TOO!
LET'S FORCE THEM IN, JAILER!
RIGHT, ANIMAL TAMER!
GO ON, ASTERIX!
RIGHT! GO ON, OBELIX!
BIFF!
WILL YOU PICK UP THE WHIP, PLEASE, ASTERIX?
GUARRRRRDS!

BIFF!
BANG!
BIFF!
AREN'T THERE ANY MORE?
THIS ISN'T THE PLACE FOR THAT KIND OF THING! IF YOU WANT TO FIGHT, GO INTO THE ARENA!
WE WANT OUR MONEY BACK!
WE WANT OUR MONEY BACK!
LISTEN TO THE CROWD! JUST LISTEN!
FOR PITY'S SAKE, GO INTO THE ARENA! THEY'LL FLATTEN THE CIRCUS! THE CIRCUS IS MY WHOLE LIFE!
OH, VERY WELL, WE'LL GO ON, BUT ONLY TO PLEASE YOU.
THANK YOU! THANK YOU! YOU WON'T REGRET IT!
?
ER... WHERE ARE THE OTHER ANIMALS?
INSIDE THAT ONE!
THIEVES! SWINDLERS! WE'LL WRECK THE CIRCUS!
BURP!

GUARDS! GET EVERYBODY OUT!
EVERYBODY OUT! EVERYBODY, BY JUPITER!
OUT! EVERYBODY OUT!
NOT US! HE DOESN'T MEAN US!
OH, SHUT UP, OBELIX!
THAT MIX-UP GAVE US GOOD COVER. WE'VE SEEN ENOUGH OF THIS PERFORMANCE. LET'S FIND A PEACEFUL SPOT TO SLEEP.
WHAT A GOOD IDEA!
WE SHOULD BE ALL RIGHT HERE. TOMORROW WE'LL THINK ABOUT OUR NEXT MOVE.
AT NIGHT THE ROMAN STREETS, INADEQUATELY PATROLLED BY THE SEBACIARIA (NIGHT WATCHMEN) ARE THE HUNTING GROUND OF SICARII, EFFRACTORES AND RAPTORES, MURDERERS, THIEVES AND MUGGERS OF ALL KINDS.
BY ALL THAT'S UNHOLY! HERE ARE TWO FINE FELLOWS SLEEPING OFF THEIR BOOZE! LET'S LIGHTEN THEIR PURSES!
RROOON!
DO YOU ROMANS NEVER SLEEP?!
BIF!

BANG!
BIF!
ER... YOU WOULDN'T BE THOSE TWO GAULS EVERYONE IS LOOKING FOR, WOULD YOU?
YES, THAT'S US. AND WHO ARE YOU?
HABEASCORPUS, CHIEF OF THE MOST FEARSOME BAND OF CUTTHROATS THE URBS HAS EVER KNOWN.
I HEAR YOU ARE MAGICIANS. YOUR STRENGTH SEEMS TO PROVE IT... WE COULD USE YOU.
WHY NOT? WE DON'T HAVE ANYWHERE TO GO.
PUT ME DOWN, THEN, AND FOLLOW ME.
LET'S GET A MOVE ON. IT'S NEARLY DAYBREAK.
HERE'S OUR HIDE-OUT: THE CATACOMBS. IT'S QUITE SAFE. YOU'LL MAKE OLD BONES DOWN HERE.
TOMORROW NIGHT WE'LL LEAVE A SKELETON STAFF HERE, AND YOU CAN TRY YOUR HAND AT SKULDUGGERY...
WE WORK AT NIGHT AND SLEEP BY DAY.
GOOD DAY, THEN!
SO THAT'S HOW IT'S DONE!

AFTER A PEACEFUL DAY, NIGHT HAS FALLEN ONCE MORE ON THE GREATEST CITY IN THE UNIVERSE *, AND SHADOWY FIGURES CREEP ALONG THE NARROW STREETS.
* ROME.
DIDO, DIDO, GIVE ME YOUR ANSWER, DO... HIC!... THERE'S AN OLD MOLA BY THE FLUMEN... HAEC! THE BELLS OF HADES GO TING-A-LING-A-... HOC!!
A DRUNK, FULL OF WINE AND GOLD! I'LL LEAVE HIM TO YOU TO SEE HOW YOU PERFORM.
RIGHT!
COME ALONG, OBELIX!
IF HE MAKES A FUSS... THE CHOP!
WE'RE NOT REALLY GOING TO GIVE HIM THE CHOP, ARE WE, ASTERIX?
OF COURSE NOT! ON THE CONTRARY WE'RE GOING TO SAVE HIM FROM THESE THUGS WATCH OUT, HERE HE COMES...
39A
LONG LIVE JULIUSH... HIC!
... CHAESHAR!
GO HOME, QUICKLY! YOU'RE IN GREAT DANGER! YOU...
METATARSUS! THE SON OF HUMERUS!
OUR COLLECTOR'S ITEMS! OUR WORKS OF ART FROM THE HOUSE OF TYPHUS!
QUICK! BEAT IT!
NOT ON YOUR LIFE! WE'LL NEVER PART AGAIN! I'LL DRINK TO THAT!
MY COLLECTOR'S ITEMS! MY OWN LITTLE WORKS OF ART! HIC!
WELL, HOW'S IT GOING? HE'LL ATTRACT THE SEBACIARA WITH ALL THAT ROW!
HE'S A FRIEND. NOBODY'S GOING TO HARM HIM!
WE'LL SOON SEE ABOUT THAT!
39B

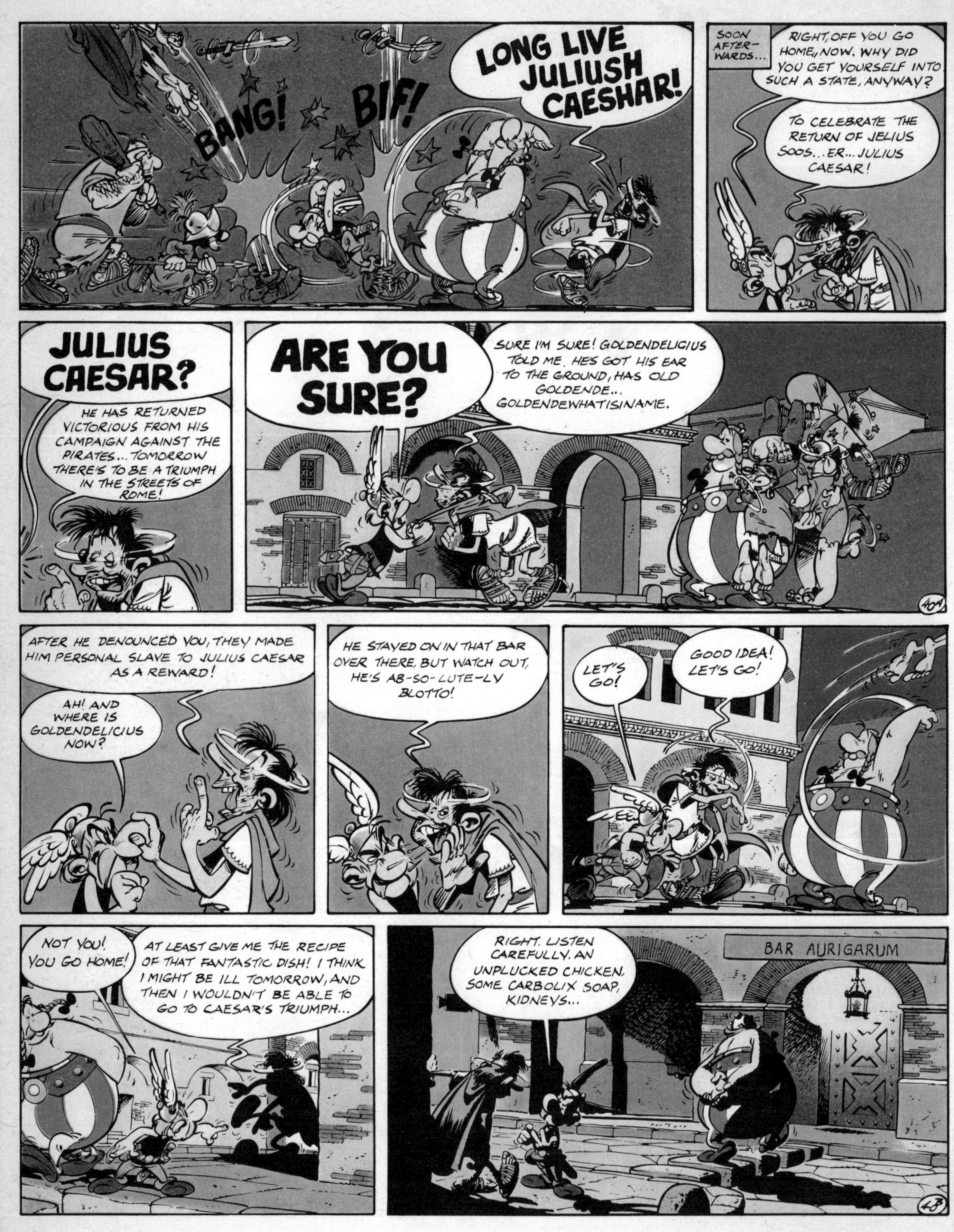
BANG!
BIF!
LONG LIVE JULIUSH CAESHAR!
SOON AFTERWARDS...
RIGHT, OFF YOU GO HOME, NOW. WHY DID YOU GET YOURSELF INTO SUCH A STATE, ANYWAY?
TO CELEBRATE THE RETURN OF JELIUS SOOS...ER...JULIUS CAESAR!
JULIUS CAESAR?
HE HAS RETURNED VICTORIOUS FROM HIS CAMPAIGN AGAINST THE PIRATES... TOMORROW THERE'S TO BE A TRIUMPH IN THE STREETS OF ROME!
ARE YOU SURE?
SURE I'M SURE! GOLDENDELICIUS TOLD ME. HE'S GOT HIS EAR TO THE GROUND, HAS OLD GOLDENDE... GOLDENDEWHATISINAME.
AFTER HE DENOUNCED YOU, THEY MADE HIM PERSONAL SLAVE TO JULIUS CAESAR AS A REWARD!
AH! AND WHERE IS GOLDENDELICIUS NOW?
HE STAYED ON IN THAT BAR OVER THERE, BUT WATCH OUT, HE'S AB-SO-LUTE-LY BLOTTO!
LET'S GO!
GOOD IDEA! LET'S GO!
NOT YOU! YOU GO HOME!
AT LEAST GIVE ME THE RECIPE OF THAT FANTASTIC DISH! I THINK I MIGHT BE ILL TOMORROW, AND THEN I WOULDN'T BE ABLE TO GO TO CAESAR'S TRIUMPH...
RIGHT. LISTEN CAREFULLY. AN UNPLUCKED CHICKEN, SOME CARBOLIX SOAP, KIDNEYS...
BAR AURIGARUM

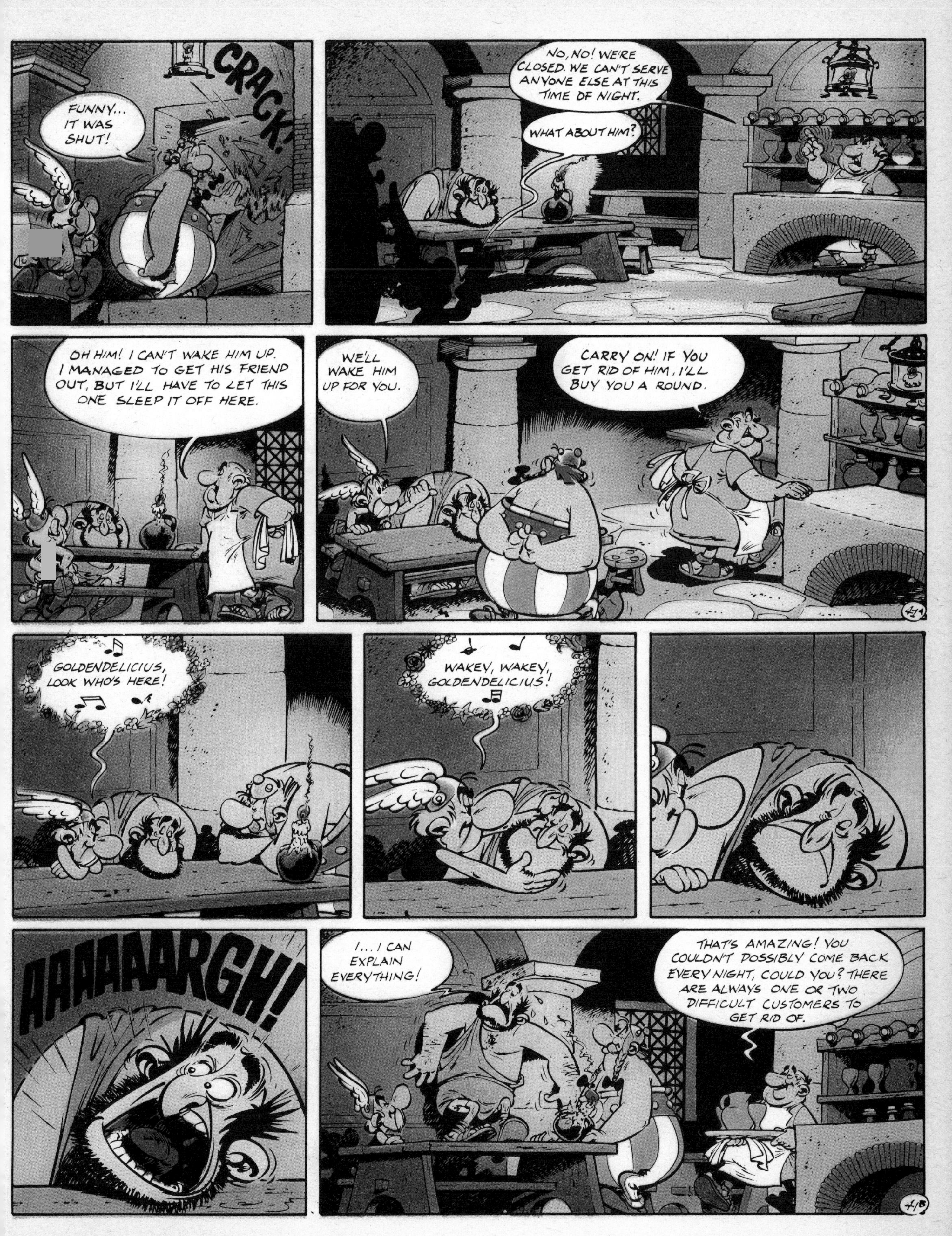
FUNNY... IT WAS SHUT!
CRACK!
NO, NO! WE'RE CLOSED. WE CAN'T SERVE ANYONE ELSE AT THIS TIME OF NIGHT.
WHAT ABOUT HIM?
OH HIM! I CAN'T WAKE HIM UP. I MANAGED TO GET HIS FRIEND OUT, BUT I'LL HAVE TO LET THIS ONE SLEEP IT OFF HERE.
WE'LL WAKE HIM UP FOR YOU.
CARRY ON! IF YOU GET RID OF HIM, I'LL BUY YOU A ROUND.
GOLDENDELICIUS, LOOK WHO'S HERE!
WAKEY, WAKEY, GOLDENDELICIUS!
AAAAAARGH!
I... I CAN EXPLAIN EVERYTHING!
THAT'S AMAZING! YOU COULDN'T POSSIBLY COME BACK EVERY NIGHT, COULD YOU? THERE ARE ALWAYS ONE OR TWO DIFFICULT CUSTOMERS TO GET RID OF.

I WAS AFRAID YOU'D TAKE MY PLACE. THAT'S WHY I DENOUNCED YOU, BUT I'M VERY SORRY, YES, I REALLY AM, VERY SORRY! YOU DON'T KNOW HOW SORRY I AM!
I HEAR YOU ARE VERY CLOSE TO CAESAR NOW?
NOT HALF! TOMORROW I SHALL RIDE IN HIS CHARIOT AT HIS TRIUMPH!
IN HIS CHARIOT?
WHENEVER THERE'S A TRIUMPH, ONE SLAVE HAS THE JOB OF HOLDING THE LAUREL WREATH ABOVE CAESAR'S HEAD TOMORROW THAT SLAVE WILL BE ME!
CAESAR'S LAUREL WREATH! THAT'S WONDERFUL, BY TOUTATIS!
YOU'RE TELLING ME! FOR A SLAVE IT'S THE CROWNING GLORY! NOW I'M A COLLECTOR'S ITEM TOO!
LANDLORD, DO YOU HAVE ANY BAY LEAVES?
NO, BUT I'VE GOT SOME PARSLEY.
THAT'LL DO. BRING IT HERE, QUICK!
YOU'RE NOT GOING TO TAKE MY PLACE, ARE YOU?
NO! IT'S THAT LAUREL WREATH WE WANT! WE'LL DO A SWAP!
I'M GOING TO TELL YOU WHAT TO DO TOMORROW... IF YOU WANT TO SEE TOMORROW, THAT IS!
I... I DON'T FEEL TOO GOOD... I'VE HAD A DROP TOO MUCH... NOW I THINK ABOUT IT, I DON'T KNOW THAT I'LL BE ABLE TO MAKE THE TRIUMPH TOMORROW...
LANDLORD! BOIL UP AN UNPLUCKED CHICKEN, SOME CARBOLIX SOAP, JAM, BLACK PEPPERCORNS, SALT, KIDNEYS, FIGS, HONEY, BLACK PUDDING, POMEGRANATE SEEDS, EGGS AND RED PEPPERS!
SHALL I PUT THE PARSLEY IN?
NO! WE'RE GOING TO MAKE WREATHS WITH THAT PARSLEY, AREN'T WE, OBELIX?
FERPECTLY RIGHT!
BANG

AT DAWN, IN A NARROW STREET NEAR CAESAR'S PALACE...
HERE HE COMES!
YOUR POTION IS ABSOLUTELY MARVELLOUS!
TAKE IT-QUICK!
CAESAR'S LAUREL WREATH!
DON'T FORGET THE PARSLEY WREATH!
IT'S A DEAL? I'LL NEVER HEAR FROM YOU AGAIN?
I PROMISE YOU THAT, BY TOUTATIS!
IT IS QUITE A GOOD TRIUMPH, AS TRIUMPHS GO... THE BOOTY ISN'T ANYTHING SPECIAL, BUT THE PRISONERS ARE PICTURESQUE...
TANTANTARA!
PARP!
TWEET TWEET!
SO THAT'S WHAT YOU MEANT WHEN YOU SAID YOU'D LEAD US TO A GREAT TRIUMPH!
...AND THE ACCLAMATIONS ARE SO DEAFENING, AND POPULAR ENTHUSIASM SO GREAT, THAT NO ONE NOTICES THAT CAESAR'S WREATH IS NOT MADE OF LAUREL...
LONG LIVE JULIUS CAESAR!
LONG LIVE CAESAR!
CAESAR!
CAESAR!
NO ONE? WELL, HARDLY ANYONE... FOR NOTHING CAN BE HIDDEN FROM THAT GREAT MAN AMONG GREAT MEN, THAT WOLF, SON OF THE ROMAN SHE-WOLF...
THAT'S FUNNY... I FEEL LIKE A PIECE OF FISH!

WELL, HOMEOPATHIX, HOW DO YOU LIKE THE TASTE OF CAESAR'S LAURELS?
YOU MAY BE RICH, BUT I BET YOU NEVER EAT ANYTHING LIKE THAT IN YOUR HOUSE!
TRUE... IT'S A BIT OVERCOOKED, AND IT WASN'T A PRIME CUT OF MEAT...
BIFF!
AND SO, IN THE GAULISH VILLAGE, UNDER A STARRY SKY, THEY CELEBRATE THE SUCCESS OF THIS EXTRAORDINARY DISH. BUT THE ADVENTURE OF ASTERIX AND OBELIX WAS TO HAVE CONSEQUENCES AS SERIOUS AS THEY WERE UNEXPECTED. FROM NOW ON, HAVING THE RECIPE FOR A REMEDY AGAINST THE EXCESSES OF DRINKING, THE ROMANS BEGAN TO INDULGE IN ORGIES OF WINE, WHICH LED TO THE DECLINE AND FALL OF THEIR EMPIRE. BE WARNED! ALCOHOL, UNLESS TAKEN IN MODERATION, IS THE FATHER OF ALL VICES... PERPECTLY TRUE!
DO YOU SING AS WELL?
THE END
UDERZO & GOSCINNY